orange -next page 3|21|16 SB

J
E
Sch

CRAWFORDSVILLE DISTRICT PUBLIC LIBRARY
222 S. WASHINGTON STREET
CRAWFORDSVILLE IND. 47933

Schubert, Ingrid, 1953-
[Woeste Willem. English]
Wild Will / by Ingrid and Dieter
Schubert. -- Minneapolis : Carolrhoda
Books, 1994.
1 v. (unpaged) : col. ill. ; 27 cm.
"First published in the Netherlands
in 1992 by Lemniscaat b.v. under the
title: Woeste Willem"--colophon.

Summary: After hearing the grouchy
retired pirate Wild Will tell stories
about treasure and the monsters he has
fought, Frank gets the idea of
accompanying Will on a return to the
sea.

ISBN 0-87614-816-X
1. Pirates-   -Fiction. I.
Schubert, Die(   )ter, 1947-   II.
Title
19 FEB 95   28633908   ICRCbp   93-2484

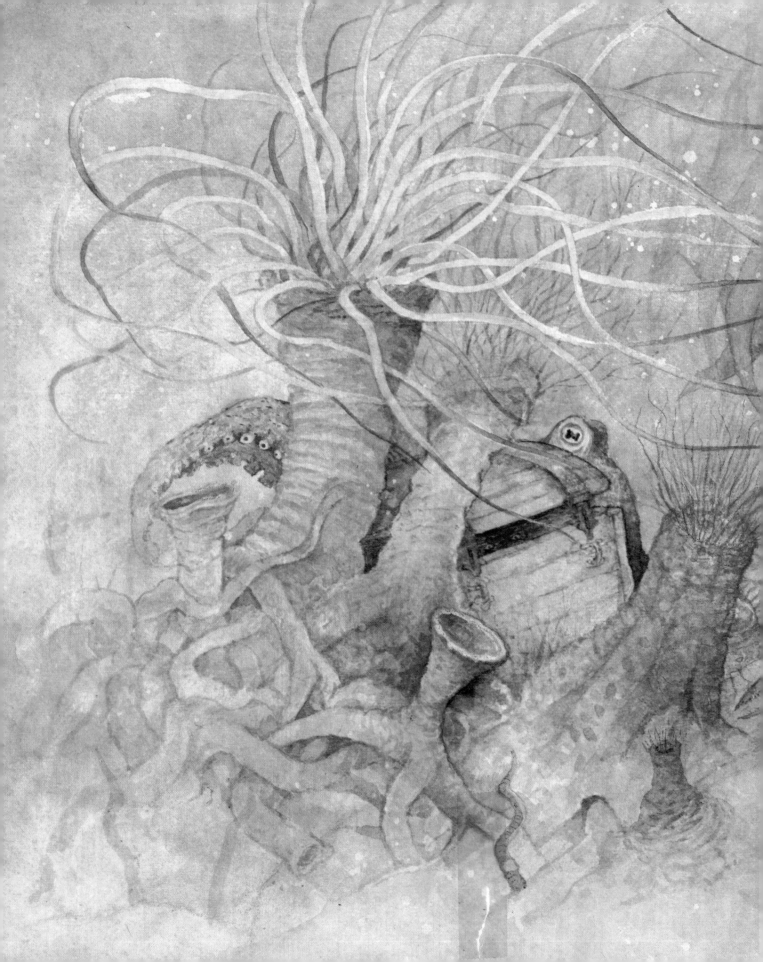

WILD WILL

by Ingrid and
Dieter Schubert

Carolrhoda Books, Inc./Minneapolis

Wild Will lives on the seashore. Will is a pirate. Well, actually, he *was* a pirate. Now he's retired. He doesn't have a ship anymore, either. Instead, he lives in a house, which he built himself.

Wild Will is a real grouch. He doesn't like company. In fact, he chases away anyone who dares to come near his house. He waves his arms and yells, "Get lost, landlubbers!"

Everyone is afraid of him. But do you think this bothers him? Not at all! He likes to be alone. All day long, he sits in the crow's nest up in the tree and peers through his telescope.

One evening when Will was sitting and playing pirate songs on his old accordion, he heard an odd noise over his head. He ran outside. To his surprise, a young boy was standing on the roof, right next to the chimney.

"Hey! You up there! Who are you? Come down here this instant!" shouted Will angrily.

"I'm Frank," said the boy, "and I can't come down. It's too high up."

"Nonsense! You got up there, didn't you? Get a move on, come down from there!"

Frank began to cry. Softly at first, then harder. What do I do now? thought Will. A kid crying on my roof—it's really more than a pirate can take.

But there was no other choice. Will had to climb up on the roof. He took Frank under his arm, and together they slid down the drainpipe.

"Boy, are you strong," said Frank when they were safely on the ground. "As strong as a lion."

"As a *sea* lion," growled Will.

"Now will you please get my kite down from the roof too?" asked Frank. "It's up there next to the chimney."

Good grief, thought Will. He wants me to go up on the roof again! Grumbling, he climbed up. There lay the kite—completely broken.

Will flung it down below. "Here you go, landlubber. Catch!"

Sadly Frank looked at his broken kite.

"And now, get lost!" roared Will.

Frank started to run. "See you!" he called over his shoulder.

"Let's hope not," Will mumbled.

But then something strange happened. Things began appearing on Will's front step. They were always little homemade things, something different every day. "Where is this junk coming from, anyway?" grumbled Will.

Then one day, he found a drawing. "Hey, that's a beautiful drawing. But wait...it's me!" Now he understood—the things were little presents for him. And he guessed right away who they were from.

"Wait now," he said to himself. "If I...yes, that's a good idea!"

Will began to rummage through his things. "I need sticks, and here, this old sheet..." He spent a whole afternoon hard at work.

At last, he was finished. He opened the door, and who do
you suppose was standing right there in front of his nose? Frank!
Will rustled the kite that he was holding behind his back.
"Guess what I have here."
"I don't have the faintest idea," said Frank.
"A kite, of course!" shouted Will. "Can't you tell?"
"A kite? But it doesn't have a tail. It won't work without a tail."

"I didn't think of that," Will had to admit.

He scratched his head. "Wait now..."

He dragged his huge pirate's chest outside. It was terribly heavy. Frank helped to lift the lid. Curious, he began to look around inside.

"What is all this?" he asked.

"Oh, this and that. All sorts of stuff. All from when I was a pirate."

Will took a strange, pointy thing out of the chest.

"Do you know what this is? This is the tooth of a flying shark. I was out on watch in a heavy storm one night when the shark came flying straight through the sail. He got stuck there. It was hard, but finally I was able to get him down. He was so grateful to me that he gave me his tooth to keep. It was already broken off, anyway."

"And this is a tiny little house that belonged to a tiny little mermaid. She gave it to me when she moved to a new one."

Frank fished something green and slippery out of the chest. "And this?"

"That's a frogman's shoe. Whenever he came to visit, I always had to swab the whole deck right away when he left. My whole ship would get soaking wet. I always told him to wring himself out before he came on board, but he still forgot."

Frank held his nose. Yecchh, the shoe stank!

"And this bottle? What goes in there?"

"That is very, very secret," said Will. "Only pirates are allowed to know that. Not you—you're a landlubber."

"I'm no landlubber. I know how to swim!"

"Well, okay, then," said Will. He tugged a piece of paper out of the bottle. "This is a treasure map. I found the treasure, but it was guarded by a gigantic sea monster. I fought that beast for hours! It had four...no, seven arms, and every time I got free of one of them, along came another. Finally I gave him a couple of good smacks on the head, and he slipped off. But he had pretty much destroyed my ship. All that was left was this board and this piece of rope. We can use it to make a tail for your kite."

But Frank had a much better plan. "Let's use your kite for a sail! We can build a new ship, then we'll go get the sea mermaid and the frogman, and fight the sea monster. Then we'll take the treasure and..."

"Well, I don't know," said Will doubtfully. "You're a landlubber, after all, and landlubbers get seasick pretty easily."

"Not me," said Frank. "I'm ready to go. I'll just get some things from home, and then I'll be right back!"

Now Will was really upset. He paced back and forth nervously. Suddenly Frank was back. He had a backpack with him. "Say, Frank," Will began, "I have to tell you something."

"Not just now," said Frank. "We don't have time now. We still have an awful lot to do."

They sawed, they hammered, they hauled—and then finally
they were finished. They were ready to put up the mast. But
Will didn't look happy at all.

"Don't you feel well?" asked Frank. "Are you seasick,
maybe?"

"No," Will said quietly. "It's something much worse."

"What is it, then? Tell me!"

"I...I can't swim."

"Is that all?" Frank laughed. "That doesn't matter."

"But what if I fall in the water?"

"No problem. I've got just the thing. Look what I have in my backpack. You can use it—I can manage without it. Now, shall we go?"

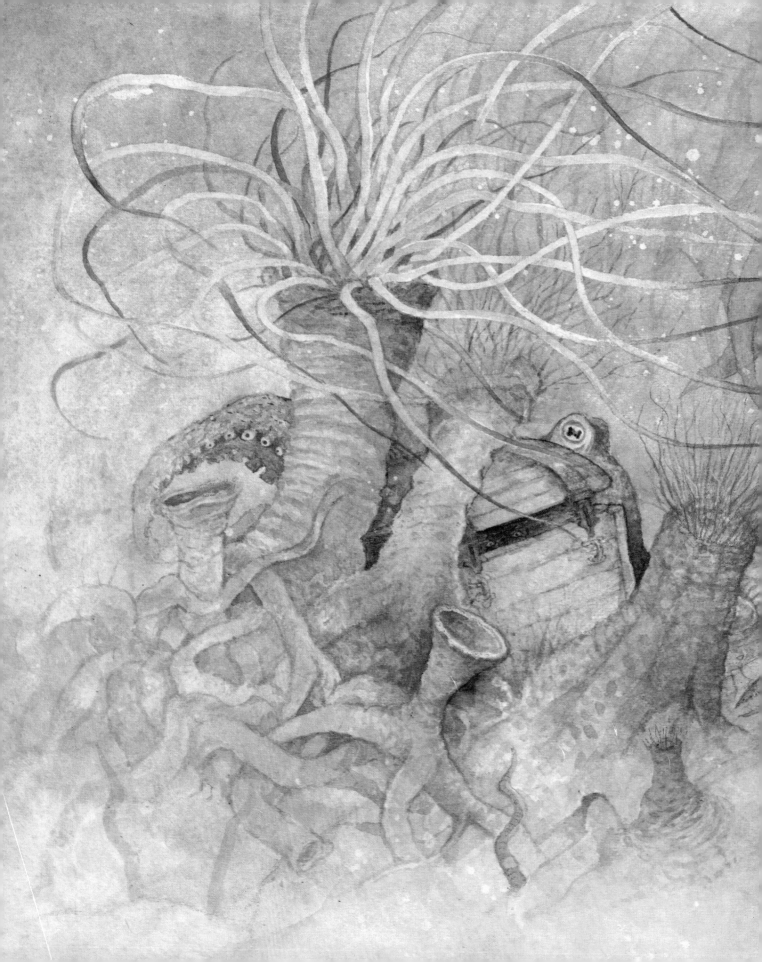

Translated from the Dutch by Amy Gelman.
English translation copyright © 1994 by Carolrhoda Books, Inc.

This edition first published 1994 by Carolrhoda Books, Inc.
First published in the Netherlands in 1992 by Lemniscaat b.v.
under the title *Woeste Willem.*
Copyright © 1992 by Lemniscaat b.v.

Library of Congress Cataloging-in-Publication Data

Schubert, Ingrid, 1953–
    [Woeste Willem. English]
    Wild Will / by Ingrid and Dieter Schubert.
        p.   cm.
    Summary: After hearing the grouchy retired pirate Wild Will
tell stories about treasure and the monsters he has fought,
Frank gets the idea of accompanying Will to the island
where the treasure lies.
    ISBN 0-87614-816-X:
    [1. Pirates—Fiction. 2.Buried treasure—Fiction.]
I. Schubert, Dieter, 1947– . II. Title.
PZ7.S3834Wi 1994
[E]—dc20   93-2484
                                                      CIP
                                                       AC

Printed in Belgium

Bound in the United States of America

1 2 3 4 5 6 – I/OS – 99 98 97 96 95 94